CONTENTS

IN THE GARDEN

Lionel was standing in the backyard
ready to start his garden.
He had big plans.
Lionel was going to plant
tomatoes for his mother,
cucumbers for his father,
green beans for his sister, Louise,
and pumpkins for himself.

Lionel imagined how much
the vegetables would grow
in a few months.
His mother could go bowling
with the tomatoes.

His father could wear the cucumbers

for shoes.

Louise could jump rope

with the green beans.

And he could make one of the pumpkins

into a clubhouse for himself.

NO LOUISES ALLOWED

But now there was work to do.

Lionel began by pulling out weeds.

He pulled and pulled and pulled
and pulled.

Some of the weeds were stubborn.

"Louise doesn't really need
green beans," said Lionel.
"And she might make me eat some.
I think I will leave them out."

Next Lionel picked up the rocks.

He bent over and over and over and over.

The rocks were getting heavy.

"Father doesn't like cucumbers

that much," he said.

"I think I will leave them out too."

Finally Lionel raked the ground
to make it level.
He raked and raked and raked
and raked.

The dirt did not move quickly.

"Big tomatoes would be very messy,"
said Lionel.

"Mother wouldn't like that.

I think I will just plant pumpkins."
Lionel bent down to scoop out
some holes for the pumpkin seeds.
There was room for a lot of holes.
"It will get too crowded here
with so many pumpkins," he said.
"I think one will be enough."

Lionel scooped out a little hole
and planted one pumpkin seed.
"How are you doing?" asked his father,
coming out the back door.
"Fine," said Lionel.

14

"I hope you didn't plant too much,"
said Father.

"It's easy to get carried away,
you know."

"Don't worry," said Lionel.

"I was very careful."

Then he went inside for lunch.

15

THE ANNIVERSARY

"Lionel, wake up!" said Louise.

Lionel rolled over in his bed.

It was still dark outside.

"Come on," said Louise.

"It's Mother and Father's anniversary.

They were married

ten years ago today."

Lionel and Louise
tiptoed down to the kitchen.
Lionel set the table for two.
"The napkin goes under the fork,
Lionel," said Louise.

"I knew that," said Lionel.

Louise poured orange juice

into two glasses.

"Don't spill it," said Lionel.

"I won't," said Louise.

She took out a frying pan

and started cooking some eggs.

"I'm making the best eggs

in the whole country," said Louise.

"So?" said Lionel.

"I'm making the best toast

in the whole world."

Louise put out the salt and pepper.

Lionel opened a jar of jam.

Soon breakfast was ready.

"The eggs look great," said Louise.

"The toast looks better," said Lionel.

They tiptoed upstairs

into their parents' bedroom.

Mother and Father were still asleep.

"Happy anniversary!"

shouted Lionel and Louise.

Mother and Father opened their eyes.

"Follow us," said Louise.

"Quickly," said Lionel.

They led the way to the kitchen.

"Look at this!" said Mother.

"Amazing," said Father.

They sat down at the table.

"I made the eggs," said Louise.

"Firm, not runny," said Father.

"Just the way I like them."

"I made the toast," said Lionel.

"Lightly browned on both sides,"
said Mother.

"Perfect for me."

Father and Mother ate everything up.

They drank their orange juice.

They used their napkins.

"That was delicious," said Mother.

"And the best part," said Father,

"is that you and Lionel

did it together."

Lionel and Louise

looked at each other.

"I guess we did," he said.

"I guess," said Louise.

Father looked at the dirty dishes.

Mother looked at the dirty pans.

"Who gets to clean up?" they asked.

"We do," said Louise,

putting the pans in the sink.

She looked at Lionel.

"And this time," she said,

"we'll really work together."

Lionel smiled and started

clearing the table.

THE MAD SCIENTIST

Outside it was raining hard.

Inside the mad scientist

Baron Von Lionel

was standing in his lab.

His monster was sitting in a chair.

The monster looked like

his friend Jeffrey.

"It is time," said the baron.

"Soon the whole world will be

under my control."

Lightning flashed in the window.

"Ha, ha, ha!"

laughed Baron Von Lionel.

The monster smiled.

He crushed a cracker in his bare hand.

The baron put some flour

in a glass of water.

Thunder rumbled overhead.

"Ho, ho, ho!"

shouted Baron Von Lionel.

The monster thumped hard

on his chest.

The baron cracked open an egg

and dropped it in the glass.

The wind whistled through the trees.

"Hee, hee, hee!"

cackled Baron Von Lionel.

The monster jumped up and down

in his chair.

The baron poured some ketchup

in the glass.

He stirred the glass three times.

"Time to drink," he told the monster.

The monster made a face.

"Noooooo!" he wailed.

"Drink," said the baron.

"I command you."

The monster shook his head.

He could be very stubborn.

"This drink will give you

super strength," said the baron.

The monster didn't care.

"I'm not going to drink that,"

he said. "I saw you make it."

"You have to drink the potion,"
said the baron.
"If you don't have super strength,
how can I rule the world?"

"You could always drink it
yourself," said the monster.
Baron Von Lionel looked
at the glass.
Little white lumps
were floating on top.
They smelled kind of funny.

"I see your point," he said.

"Super strength will have to wait."

Outside it was still raining hard.

But the world was safe for

another day.

SPRING CLEANING

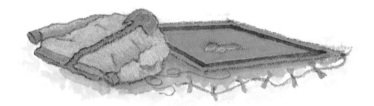

Everyone was cleaning the house.

Mother was washing the windows.

Father was washing the floors.

Lionel and Louise were shaking out

the rugs.

"That's good," said Mother

when they were done.

"Now we have to get rid of

some things."

"Like what?" asked Lionel.

"Things we don't use or need,"
said Father.

"Junk," said Louise.

Mother threw out a broken vase
she had been meaning to fix
for two years.

Father threw out

some old magazines.

Louise threw out

a poster of a rock star

she didn't like anymore.

Lionel looked carefully through
his room.

He checked in his closet
and under the bed.

He found nothing to throw out.

"Hurry up, Lionel," said Louise.

"Get rid of something."

She took out his old jacket.

"How about this?" she asked.

"It doesn't fit you now

and the sleeve is ripped."

"I want to keep it,"

said Lionel.

That was his lucky jacket.

He had once found a dollar

while wearing it.

"What about this kite?" asked Louise.

"There's a big hole in the middle."

Lionel shook his head.

That was the first kite he had

ever made.

Nobody had thought it would fly.

But Lionel had made the kite soar.

"What's going on?"

asked Father and Mother.

"Lionel won't throw anything out,"

said Louise.

"Everything I have is important,"
said Lionel.

"Everything reminds me of something."

Mother nodded. "I understand,"
she said. "But you can't
keep everything, Lionel.
Your life will get too crowded."

Lionel pictured jackets piled up

in front of his windows.

He saw kites covering the floor.

"You don't throw out

the memories," said Father.

"You keep them for always."

Lionel nodded.

Then he put the jacket on top of

Louise's poster.

"Good-bye, jacket," he said.

"What about the kite?"

asked Louise.

Lionel held it firmly.

"The kite," he said,

"can wait till next year."